The Tale of the Unknown Island

José Saramago

The Tale
of the
Unknown Island

ILLUSTRATIONS BY PETER SÍS

Translated from the Portuguese by
Margaret Jull Costa

HARCOURT BRACE & COMPANY
New York   San Diego   London

Requests for permission to make copies of any part
of the work should be mailed to the following address:
Permissions Department, Harcourt, Inc., 6277 Sea Harbor Drive,
Orlando, Florida 32887-6777.

This is a translation of•*O Conto da Ilha Desconhecida*.

Library of Congress Cataloging-in-Publication Data
Saramago, José.
[Conto da ilha desconhecida. English]
The tale of the unknown island/José Saramago: illustrated by
Peter Sís: translated from the Portuguese by Margaret Jull Costa.
p.   cm.
ISBN 0-15-100595-8
I. Costa, Margaret Jull. II. Title.
PQ9281.A66C6613   1999
869.3'42—dc21   99-31111

Designed by Lori McThomas Buley
Text set in Centaur MT
Printed in Mexico
First edition
A C E D B

The Tale of the Unknown Island

A MAN WENT TO KNOCK AT THE KING'S DOOR AND said, Give me a boat. The king's house had many other doors, but this was the door for petitions. Since the king spent all his time sitting at the door for favors (favors being offered to the king, you understand), whenever he heard someone knocking at the door for petitions, he would pretend not to hear, and only when the continuous pounding of the bronze doorknocker became not just deafening, but positively scandalous, disturbing the peace of the neighborhood (people would start muttering, What kind of king is he if he won't even answer the door), only then would he order the first secretary to go and find out what the supplicant wanted, since there seemed no way of silencing him. Then, the first secretary would call the second secretary, who would call the third secretary, who would give orders to the first assistant who would, in turn, give orders to the second assistant, and so on all the way down the line to the cleaning woman, who, having no one else to give orders to, would half-open the door and ask through the crack, What do you want. The supplicant would state his business, that is, he would ask what he had come to ask, then he would wait by the door for his request to trace the path back, person by person, to the king. The king, occupied as usual with the favors being offered him, would take a long time to reply, and it was no small measure of his concern for the happiness and well-being of his people that he would, finally, resolve to ask the first secretary for an authoritative opinion in writing, the first secretary, needless to say, would pass on the command to the second secretary, who would pass it to the third secretary, and so on down once again to the cleaning woman, who would give a yes or a no depending on what kind of mood she was in.

However, in the case of the man who wanted a boat, this is not quite what happened. When the cleaning woman asked him through the crack in the door, What do you want, the man, unlike all the others, did not ask for a title, a medal, or simply money, he said, I want to talk to the king, You know perfectly well that the king can't come, he's busy at the door for favors, replied the woman, Well, go and tell him that I'm not leaving here until he comes, in person, to find out what I want, said the man, and he lay down across the threshold, covering himself with a blanket against the cold. Anyone wanting to go in or out would have to step over him first. Now this posed an enormous problem, because one must bear in mind that, according to the protocol governing the different doors, only one supplicant could be dealt with at a time, which meant that, as long as there was someone waiting there for a response, no one else could approach and make known their needs or ambitions. At first glance, it would seem that the person to gain most from this article in the regulations was the king, given that the fewer people bothering him with their various tales of woe, the longer he could spend, undisturbed, receiving, relishing and piling up favors. A second glance, however, would reveal that the king was very much the loser, because when people realized the unconscionable amount of time it took to get a reply, the ensuing public protests would serious- ly increase social unrest, and that, in turn, would have an immediate and negative effect on the flow

of favors being offered to the king. In this particular case, as a result of weighing up the pros and cons, after three days, the king went, in person, to the door for favors to find out what he wanted, this troublemaker who had refused to allow his request to go through the proper bureaucratic channels. Open the door, said the king to the cleaning woman, and she said, Wide open, or just a little bit. The king hesitated for a moment, the fact was that he did not much care to expose himself to the air of the streets, but then, he reflected, it would look bad, unworthy of his majestic self, to speak to one of his subjects through a crack in the door, as if he were afraid of him, especially with someone else listening in to the conversation, a cleaning woman who would immediately go and tell all and sundry who knows what, Wide open, he ordered. The moment he heard the bolts being drawn back, the man who wanted a boat got up from the step by the door, folded his blanket and waited. These signs that someone was finally going to deal with the matter, which meant that the space by the door would therefore soon be free, brought together a number of other aspiring recipients of the king's generosity who were hanging about nearby ready to claim the place as soon as it became vacant. The unexpected arrival of the king (such a thing had never happened for as long as he had worn the crown) provoked enormous surprise, not only among the aforementioned candidates, but also among the people living on the other side of the street who, attracted by the sudden commotion, were leaning out of their windows. The only person who was not particularly surprised was the man who had come to ask for a boat. He had calculated, and his prediction was proving correct, that the king, even if it took him three days, was bound to be curious to see the face of the person who, for no apparent reason and with extraordinary boldness, had demanded to speak to him. Thus, torn between his own irresistible curiosity and his displeasure at seeing so many people gathered together all at once, the king very ungraciously fired off three questions one after the other, What do you want, Why didn't you say what you wanted straightaway, Do you imagine I have nothing better to do, but the man only answered the first question, Give me a boat, he said. The king was so taken aback that the cleaning woman hurriedly offered him the chair with the straw seat that she herself used to sit on when she had some needlework to do, for, as well as cleaning, she was also responsible for minor sewing chores in the palace, for example, darning the pages' socks. Feeling somewhat awkward, for the chair was much lower than his throne, the king was trying to find the best way to

arrange his legs, first drawing them in, then letting them splay out to either side, while the man who wanted the boat patiently waited for the next question, And may one know what you want this boat for, was what the king did in fact ask when he had finally managed to install himself with a reasonable degree of comfort on the cleaning woman's chair, To go in search of the unknown island, replied the man, What unknown island, asked the king, suppressing his laughter, as if he had before him one of those utter madmen obsessed with sea voyages, whom it would be as well not to cross, at least not straightaway, The unknown island, the man said again, Nonsense, there are no more unknown islands, Who told you, sir, that there are no more unknown islands, They're all on the maps, Only the known islands are on the maps, And what is this unknown island you want to go in search of, If I could tell you that, it wouldn't be unknown, Have you heard someone talking about it, asked the king, more serious now, No, no one, In that case, why do you insist that it exists, Simply because there can't possibly not be an unknown island, And you came here to ask me for a boat, Yes, I came here to ask you for a boat, And who are you that I should give you a boat, And who are you to refuse me one, I am the king of this kingdom, and all the boats in the kingdom belong to me, You belong to them far more than they belong to you, What do you mean, asked the king, troubled, I mean that without them you're nothing, whereas, without you, they can still set sail, Under my orders, with my pilots and my sailors, But I'm not asking you for sailors or a pilot, all I'm asking you for is a boat, And what about this unknown island, if you find it, will it be mine, You, sir, are only interested in islands that are already known, And unknown ones too, once they're known, Perhaps this one won't let itself be known, Then I won't give you the boat, Yes, you will. When they heard these words, uttered with such calm confidence, the would-be supplicants at the door for favors, whose impatience had been growing steadily since this conversation had begun, decided to intervene in the man's favor, more out of a desire to get rid of him than out of any sense of solidarity, and so they started shouting, Give him the boat, give him the boat. The king opened his mouth to tell the cleaning woman to call the palace guard to come and reestablish public order and impose discipline, but, at that moment, the people watching from the windows of the houses opposite enthusiastically joined in the chorus, shouting along with the others, Give him the boat, give him the boat. Faced by such an unequivocal expression of the popular will and worried about what he might have missed meanwhile at the door for favors, the king raised his right hand to command silence and said, I'm going to give you a boat, but you'll have to find your own crew, I need all my sailors for the known islands. The cheers from the crowd drowned out the man's words of thanks, besides, judging from the movements of his lips, he might just as easily have been saying, Thank you, my lord, as Don't worry, I'll manage, but everyone clearly heard what the king said next, Go down to the docks, ask to speak to the harbor-master, tell him I sent you, and that he is to give you a boat, take my card with you. The man who was to be given a boat read the visiting card, which bore the word King underneath the king's name, and these were the words the king had written as he rested the card on the cleaning woman's shoulder, Give the bearer a boat, it doesn't have to be a large boat, but it should be a

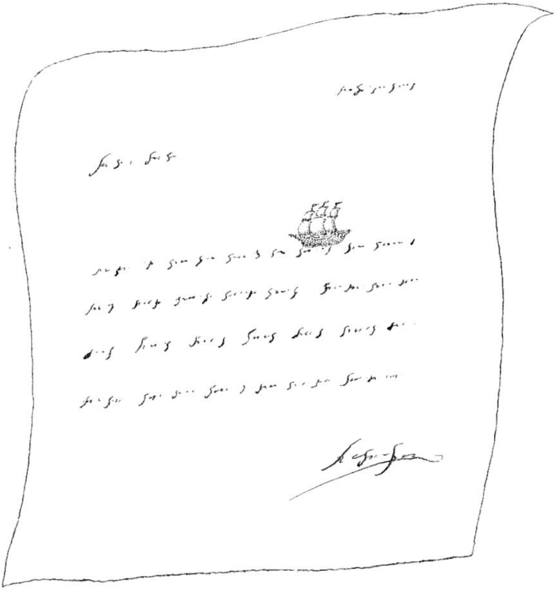

safe, seaworthy boat, I don't want to have him on my conscience if things should go wrong. When the man looked up, this time, one imagines, in order to say thank you for the gift, the king had already withdrawn, and only the cleaning woman was there, looking at him thoughtfully. The man moved away from the door, a signal for the other supplicants finally to approach, there is little point in describing the ensuing confusion, with everyone trying to get to the door first, but alas, the door was once more closed. They banged the bronze doorknocker again to summon the cleaning woman, but the cleaning woman wasn't there, she had turned and left, with her bucket and her broom, by another door, the door of decisions, which is rarely used, but when it is used, it decidedly is. Now one can understand the thoughtful look on the cleaning woman's face, for it was at that precise moment that she had decided to go after the man as he set off to the port to take possession of the boat. She decided that she had had enough of a life spent cleaning and scrubbing palaces, that it was time to change jobs, that cleaning and scrubbing boats was her true vocation, at least she would never lack for water at sea. The man has no idea that, even though he has not yet started recruiting crew members, he is already being followed by the person who will be in charge of swabbing down the decks and of other such cleaning tasks, indeed, this is the way fate usually treats us, it's there right behind us, it has already reached out a hand to touch us on the shoulder while we're still muttering to ourselves, It's all over, that's it, who cares anyhow.

After walking quite a way, the man reached the harbor, went down to the dock, asked for the harbormaster and, while he was waiting for him, set to wondering which of the boats moored there would be his, he knew it wouldn't be large, the king's visiting card was very clear on that point, that excluded the steamships, cargo ships and warships, nor could it be so small that it would not withstand the battering winds or the rigors of the sea, the king had been categorical on that point too, It should be a safe, seaworthy boat, those had been his actual words, thus implicitly excluding rowboats, barges and dinghies, which, although entirely seaworthy and safe, each in its own way, were not made to plough the oceans, which is where one finds unknown islands. A short way away, hidden behind some barrels, the cleaning woman ran her eyes over the moored boats, I fancy that one, she thought, not that her opinion counted, she hadn't even been hired, but first, let's hear what the harbormaster has to say. The harbormaster came, read the card, looked the man up and down, and asked the question the king had

neglected to ask, Do you know how to sail, have you got a master's ticket, to which the man replied, I'll learn at sea. The harbormaster said, I wouldn't recommend it, I'm a sea captain myself and I certainly wouldn't venture out to sea in just any old boat, Then give me one I could venture out in, no, not one like that, give me a boat I can respect and that will respect me, That's sailor's talk, yet you're not a sailor, If I talk like a sailor, then I must be one. The harbormaster reread the king's visiting card, then asked, Can you tell me why you want the boat, To go in search of the unknown island, There are no unknown islands left, That's just what the king said to me, He learned everything he knows about islands from me, It's odd that you, a man of the sea, should say to me that there are no unknown islands left, I'm a man of the land and yet I know that even known islands remain unknown until we set foot on them, But, if I understood you right, you're going in search of one that no one has set foot on, Yes, I'll know it when I get there, If you get there, Well, boats do get wrecked along the way, but if that should happen to me, you must write in the harbor records that I reached such and such a point, You mean that you always reach somewhere, You wouldn't be the man you are if you didn't know that. The harbormaster said, I'm going to give you the boat you need, Which one, It's a very experienced boat, dating from the days when everyone was off searching for unknown islands, Which one, Indeed it may even have found some, Which is it, That one. As soon as the cleaning woman saw where the harbormaster was pointing, she emerged from behind the barrels, shouting, That's my boat, that's my boat, one must forgive her unusual and entirely unjustifiable claim of ownership, the boat just happened to be

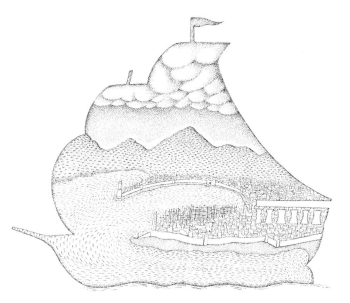

the one she had liked too. It looks like a caravel, said the man, It is more or less, agreed the harbormaster, it started life as a caravel, then underwent various repairs and modifications that altered it a bit, But it's still a caravel, Yes, it's pretty much kept its original character, And it's got masts and sails, That's what you need when you go in search of unknown islands. The cleaning woman could contain herself no longer, As far as I'm concerned, that's the boat for me, And who are you, asked the man, Don't you remember me, No, I don't, I'm the cleaning woman, Cleaning what, The king's palace, The woman who opened the door for petitions, The very same, And why aren't you back at the king's palace cleaning and opening doors, Because the doors I really wanted to open have already been opened and because, from now on, I will only clean boats, So you want to go with me in search of the unknown island, I left the palace by the door of decisions, In that case, go and have a look at the caravel, after all this time, it must be in need of a good wash, but watch out for the seagulls, they're not to be trusted, Don't you want to come with me and see what your boat is like inside, You said it was your boat, Sorry about that, I only said it because I liked it, Liking is probably the best form of ownership, and ownership the worst form of liking. The harbormaster interrupted their conversation, I have to hand over the keys to the owner of the ship, which of you is it to be, it's up to you, I don't care either way, Do boats have keys, asked the man, Not to get in with, no, but there are store cupboards and lockers, and the captain's desk with the logbook, I'll leave it all up to her, I'm going to find a crew, said the man and walked off.

The cleaning woman went to the harbormaster's office to collect the keys, then she boarded the boat, where two things proved useful to her, the palace broom and the warning about the seagulls, she was only halfway up the gangplank joining the side of the ship to the quay when the wretches hurled themselves upon her, screaming furiously, beaks open, as if they wanted to devour her on the spot. They didn't know who they were dealing with. The cleaning woman set down the bucket, slipped the keys down her cleavage, steadied herself on the gangplank and, whirling the broom about her as if it were a broadsword of old, managed to scatter the murderous band. It was only when she actually boarded the ship that she understood the seagulls' anger, there were nests everywhere, many of them abandoned, others still with eggs in them, and a few with nestlings waiting, mouths agape, for food, That's all very well, but you're going to have to move house, a ship about to set sail in search of the unknown island can't leave looking like a henhouse, she said. She threw the empty nests into the water, but left the others where they were for the moment. Then she rolled up her sleeves and started scrubbing the deck. When she had finished this arduous task, she went and opened the sail lockers and began carefully examining the sails to see what state the seams were in after so long without going to sea and without being stretched by the vigorous winds. The sails are the muscles of the boat, you just have to see them swelling and straining in the wind to know that, but, like all muscles, if they're not used regularly, they grow weak, flabby, sinew-less. And the seams are like the sinews of the sails, thought the cleaning woman, glad to find she was picking up the art of seamanship so quickly. Some seams were fraying, and these she carefully marked, since the needle and thread which, only yesterday, she had used to darn the pages' socks,

would not suffice for this work. The other lockers, she soon discovered, were empty. The fact that there was no gunpowder in the gunpowder locker, just a bit of black dust in the bottom, which she at first took to be mouse droppings, did not bother her in the least, indeed there is no law, at least not to the knowledge of a cleaning woman, that going in search of an unknown island must necessarily be a warlike enterprise. What did greatly annoy her was the complete absence of food rations in the food locker, not for her own sake, for she was more than used to the meager pickings at the palace, but because of the man to whom this boat was given, the sun will soon be going down, and he'll be back clamoring for food, as all men do the moment they get home, as if they were the only ones who had a stomach and a need to fill it, And if he brings sailors back with him to crew the ship, they've always got monstrous appetites, and then, said the cleaning woman, I don't know how we'll manage.

She needn't have worried. The sun had just vanished into the ocean when the man with the boat appeared at the far end of the quay. He was carrying a package in his hand, but he was alone and looked dispirited. The cleaning woman went to wait for him by the gangplank, but before she could open her mouth to find out how the rest of the day had gone, he said, Don't worry, I've brought enough food for both of us, And the sailors, she asked, No one came, as you can see, But did some at least say they would come, she asked, They said there are no more unknown islands and that, even if there were, they weren't prepared to leave the comfort of their homes and the good life on board passenger ships just to get involved in some oceangoing adventure, looking for the impossible, as if we were still living in the days when the sea was dark, And what did you say to them, That the sea is always dark, And you didn't tell them about the unknown island, How could I tell them about an unknown island, if I don't even know where it is, But you're sure it exists, As sure as I am that the sea is dark, Right now, seen from up here, with the water the color of jade and the sky ablaze, it doesn't seem at all dark to me, That's just an illusion, sometimes islands seem to float above the surface of the water, but it's not true, How do you think you'll manage if you haven't got a crew, I don't know yet, We could live here, and I could get work cleaning the boats that come into port, and you, And I, You must have some skill, a craft, a profession, as they call it nowadays, I have, did have, will have if necessary, but I want to find the unknown island, I want to find out who I am when I'm there on that island, Don't you know, If you don't step outside yourself, you'll never discover who you are, The king's philosopher, when he had nothing to do, would come and sit beside me and watch me darning the pages' socks, and sometimes he would start philosophizing, he used to say that each man is an island, but since that had nothing to do with me, being a woman, I paid no attention to him, what do you think, That you have to leave the island in order to see the island, that we can't see ourselves unless we become free of ourselves, Unless we escape from ourselves, you mean, No, that's not the same thing. The blaze in the sky was dying down, the waters grew suddenly purple, now not even the cleaning woman could doubt that the sea really is dark, at least at certain times of the day. The man said, Let's leave the philoso-phizing to the king's philosopher, that's what they pay him for after all, and let's eat, but the woman did not agree, First, you've got to inspect your

boat, you've only seen it from the outside, What sort of state did you find it in, Well, some of the seams on the sails need reinforcing, Did you go down into the hold, has the ship let in much water, There's a bit in the bottom, sloshing about with the ballast, but that seems normal, it's good for the boat, How did you learn these things, I just did, But how, The same way you told the harbormaster that you would learn to sail, at sea, We're not at sea yet, We're on the water though, My belief was that, with sailing, there are only two true teachers, one is the sea and the other the boat, And the sky, you're forgetting the sky, Yes, of course, the sky, The winds, The clouds, The sky, Yes, the sky.

It took them less than a quarter of an hour to go round the whole ship, a caravel, even a converted one, doesn't really allow for long walks. It's lovely, said the man, but if I can't get enough crew members to work it, I'll have to go back to the king and tell him I don't want it any more, Honestly, the first obstacle you come across and you lose heart, The first obstacle was having to wait three days for the king and I didn't give up then, If we can't find sailors willing to come with us, then we'll have to manage alone, You're mad, two people on their own couldn't possibly sail a ship like this, why, I'd have to be at the helm all the time, and you, well, I couldn't even begin to explain, it's madness, We'll see, now let's go and eat. They went up to the quarterdeck, the man still protesting at what he called her madness, and there the cleaning woman opened the package he had brought, a loaf of bread, hard goat's cheese, olives and a bottle of wine. The moon was now but a hand's breadth above the sea, the shadows cast by the yard and the mainmast came and lay at their feet. Our caravel's really lovely, said the woman,

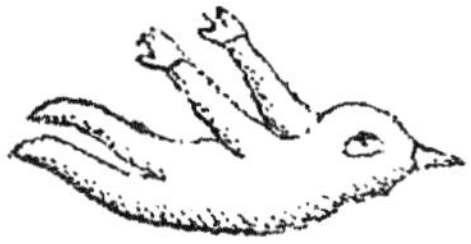

then corrected herself, I mean your caravel, It won't be mine for very long I shouldn't think, Whether you sail it or not, it's yours, the king gave it to you, Yes, but I asked him to give it to me so that I could go in search of an unknown island, But these things don't just happen from one moment to the next, it all takes time, my grandfather always used to say that anyone going to sea must make his preparations on land first, and he wasn't even a sailor, With no crew members we can't sail, So you said, And we'll have to provision the ship with the thousand and one things you need for a voyage like this, given that we don't know where it might lead us, Of course, and then we'll have to wait for the right season, and leave on a good tide, and have people come to the quay to wish us a safe journey, You're making fun of me, Not at all, I would never make fun of the person who got me to leave the palace by the door

of decisions, Forgive me, And I won't go back through that door whatever happens. The moonlight was falling directly on the cleaning woman's face, Lovely, really lovely, thought the man, and this time he didn't mean the caravel. The woman did not think anything, she must have thought all she had to think in those three days during which she would open the door now and then to see if he was still out there, waiting. There wasn't a crumb of bread or cheese left, not a drop of wine, they had thrown the olive stones into the sea, the deck was as clean as it had been when the cleaning woman had wiped a cloth over it for the last time. A steamship's siren let out a potent growl, such as leviathans must have made, and the woman said, When it's our turn, we won't make so much noise about it. Although they were still in the harbor, the water lapped slightly as the steamship passed, and the man said, But we'll certainly sway about a lot more. They both laughed, then fell silent, after a while, one of them suggested that perhaps they should go to sleep, Not that I'm particularly sleepy, and the other agreed, No, I'm not either, then they fell silent again, the moon rose and continued to rise, at one point, the woman said, There are bunks down below, the man said, Yes, and that was when they got up and went below decks, where the woman said, See you tomorrow, I'm going this way, and the man replied, I'm going this way, see you tomorrow, they did not say port or starboard, probably because they were both new to the art. The woman turned back, Oh, I forgot, and she took two candle stumps out of her apron pocket, I found them when I was cleaning, but I don't have any matches, I do, said the man. She held the candles, one in each hand, he lit a match, then, protecting the flame beneath the dome of his cupped fingers, he carefully applied it to the old wicks, the flame took, grew slowly like the moonlight, lit the face of the cleaning woman, there's no need to say what he thought, She's lovely, but what she thought was this, He's obviously got eyes only for the unknown island, just one example of how people can misinterpret the look in another person's eyes, especially when they've only just met. She handed him a candle, said, See you tomorrow, then, sleep well, he wanted to say the same thing, only differently, Sweet dreams, was the phrase he came out with, in a little while, when he is down below, lying on his bunk, other phrases will spring to mind, wittier, more charming, as such phrases should be when a man finds himself alone with a woman. He wondered if she would already be asleep, if it had taken her long to fall asleep, then he imagined that he was looking for her and couldn't find her anywhere, that the two of them were lost on a vast ship, sleep is a skilled magician, it changes the proportions of things, the distances between them, it separates people and they're lying next to each other, brings them together and they can barely see one another, the woman is sleeping only a few yards away from him and he cannot reach her, yet it's so very easy to go from port to starboard.

He had wished her sweet dreams, but he was the one who spent all night dreaming. He dreamed that his caravel was on the high seas, with the three lateen sails gloriously full, cutting a path through the waves, while he controlled the ship's wheel and the crew rested in the shade. He couldn't understand what these sailors were doing there, the same ones who had refused to embark with him to go in search of the unknown island, they probably regretted the crude irony with which they had treated him. He could see animals wandering the deck too, ducks, rabbits, chickens, the usual domestic livestock, pecking at the grains of corn or nibbling on the cabbage leaves that a sailor was throwing to them, he couldn't remember bringing them on board, but however it had happened, it was only natural they should be there, for what if the unknown island turned out to be a desert island, as had so often been the case in the past, it was best to play it safe, and we all know that opening the door to the rabbit hutch and lifting a rabbit out by the ears is always easier than having to pursue it over hill and dale. From the depths of the hold he could hear a chorus of neighing horses, lowing oxen, braying donkeys, the voices of the noble beasts so vital for carrying out heavy work, and how did they get there, how can they possibly fit into a caravel which has barely enough room for the human crew, suddenly the wind veered, the mainsail flapped and rippled, and behind was something he hadn't noticed before, a group of women, who, even without counting, must be as numerous as the sailors and are occupied in womanly tasks, the time had not yet come for them to occupy themselves with other things, it's obvious that this must be a dream, no one in real life ever traveled like this. The man at the ship's wheel looked for the cleaning woman, but couldn't see her, Perhaps she's in the bunk to starboard, resting after scrubbing the deck, he thought, but he was deceiving himself, because he knows perfectly well, although again he doesn't know how he knows, that, at the last moment, she chose not to come, that she jumped onto the quay, shouting, Goodbye, goodbye, since you only have eyes for the unknown island, I'm leaving, and it wasn't true, right now his eyes are searching for her and do not find her. At that moment, the sky clouded over and it began to

rain, and, having rained, innumerable plants began to sprout from the rows of sacks filled with earth lined up along the bulwarks, they are there not because of fears that there will not be enough soil on the unknown island, but because in that way one can gain time, the day we arrive, all we will have to do is transplant the fruit trees, sow the seeds from the miniature wheat fields ripening here, and decorate the flower beds with the flowers that will bloom from these buds. The man at the wheel asks the sailors resting on the deck if they can see any uninhabited islands yet, and they say they can see no islands at all, uninhabited or otherwise, but that they are considering disembarking on the first bit of inhabited land that appears, as long as there is a port where the ship can anchor, a tavern where they can drink and a bed to frolic in, since there's no room to do so here, with so many people crowded together.

But what about the unknown island, asked the man at the wheel, The unknown island doesn't exist, except as an idea in your head, the king's geographers went to look at the maps and declared that it's been years since there have been any unknown islands, You should have stayed in the city, then, instead of hindering my voyage, We were looking for a better place to live and decided to take advantage of your journey, You're not sailors, We never were, I won't be able to sail this ship all alone, You should have thought of that before asking the king to give it to you, the sea won't teach you how to sail. Then the man at the wheel saw land in the distance and tried to sail straight past, pretending that it was the mirage of another land, an image that had traveled across space from the other side of the world, but the men who had never been sailors protested, they said that was where they wanted to disembark,

This island's on the map, they cried, we'll kill you if you don't take us there. Then, of its own accord, the caravel turned its prow toward land, entered the port and drew alongside the quay, You can leave, said the man at the wheel, and they immediately all trooped off, first the women, then the men, but they did not leave alone, they took with them the ducks, the rabbits and the chickens, they took the oxen, the donkeys and the horses, and even the seagulls, one after the other, flew off, leaving the boat behind, carrying their nestlings in their beaks, something never seen before, but there's always a first time. The man at the wheel watched this exodus in silence, he did nothing to hold back those who were abandoning him, at least they had left him the trees, the wheat and the flowers, as well as the climbing plants that were twining round the masts and festooning the ship's sides. In the rush to leave, the sacks of earth had

split and spilled open, so that the whole deck had become a field, dug and sown, with just a little more rain there should be a good harvest. Ever since the voyage to the unknown island began, we have not seen the man at the wheel eat, that must be because he is dreaming, just dreaming, and if in his dreams he fancies a bit of bread or an apple, it would be pure invention, nothing more. The roots from the trees are now penetrating the frame of the ship itself, it won't be long before these hoisted sails cease to be needed, the wind will just have to catch the crown of the trees and the caravel will set off for its destination. It is a forest that sails and bobs upon the waves, a forest where, quite how no one knows, birds have begun to sing, they must have been hidden somewhere and suddenly decided to emerge into the light, perhaps because the wheat field is ripening and needs harvesting. Then the man locked the ship's wheel and went down to the field with a sickle in his hand, and when he had cut down the first few ears, he saw a shadow beside his shadow. He woke up with his arms about the cleaning woman, and her arms about him, their bodies and their bunks fused into one, so that no one can tell any more if this is port or starboard. Then, as soon as the sun had risen, the man and the woman went to paint in white letters on both sides of the prow the name that the caravel still lacked. Around midday, with the tide, The Unknown Island finally set to sea, in search of itself.

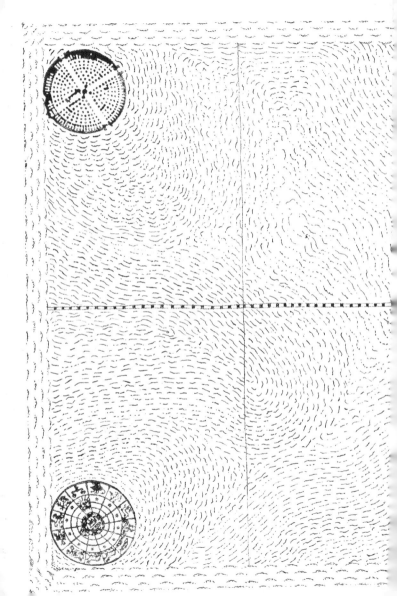